# LiTTLE PASSPORTS®

# Awakening the Dragon

Written by AnnMarie Anderson

Illustrated by Carrie English

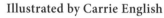

10

## Sam & Sofia's Scooter Stories

First paperback edition printed in 2022 by Little Passports, Inc.
Copyright © 2022 Little Passports
All rights reserved
Cover illustration by Rhiannon Davenport
Made in China, Shenzhen
10 9 8 7 6 5 4 3 2 1

Little Passports, Inc.
27 Maiden Lane, Suite 400, San Francisco, CA 94108
www.littlepassports.com
ISBN: 978-1-953148-12-4

# Contents

# 1

# Kayak Explorers

Sam dipped his paddle into the water and steered away from the shore.

"Whoa!" he cried as the kayak wobbled.

"No worries, Sam. I got it."

Sofia steadied the boat she and Sam shared.

"Great work," their guide Janine said from her kayak. "You two are working well together!"

Suddenly there was a splash beside them. Sam turned to see his friends Mikey and Ellie in the next boat.

"Whoops!" Ellie said. "I dropped it!"

Janine nimbly dipped her paddle into the water and spun her kayak around. She paddled over to help Ellie retrieve her paddle from the bay with just a few long strokes.

"Wow," Sam said softly. "Impressive!"

Meanwhile, the boat he shared with Sofia bobbled a bit and then got stuck in a tangle of tall seagrass growing along the shore.

"This is so fun," Sofia said with a giggle as she steered the boat away from the grass.

"Um, yeah," Sam replied, following Sofia's lead. He gripped his paddle tightly as the boat wavered again.

Sam's aunt Charlie floated by, smiling.

"You've got it, Sam," she called out. "Just keep calm and kayak on! There's so much wildlife to see in these wetlands."

Sam kept his eyes peeled, being careful not to make big splashes as he paddled. Suddenly, he spotted a tall grayish-blue long-legged bird with a bearded fringe of wispy white feathers standing statue-like in the bay.

"Look!" he called out softly, pointing at the bird.

Janine returned Ellie's lost paddle and floated back toward Sam and Sofia. "That's a great blue heron," she said, pulling out her binoculars. "Isn't it beautiful?"

"I'd love to take a picture," Sam whispered to Sofia. "But I'm scared to put down my paddle and pick up the camera. What if we tip?"

"I'll keep the boat steady for you," Sofia said.

"Okay," Sam agreed reluctantly. "But this is my favorite camera. I don't want it to go for a swim!"

Still, Sam really wanted that photo! He carefully placed his paddle across his lap and ever so slowly lifted his camera from its strap around his neck.

## Click-click!

"You've got it, Sam," Sofia said encouragingly.

As Sam snapped away, the kayak teetered from side to side.

"Yikes!" he gasped. Sam's paddle began to slip off his lap, but he grabbed it just in time, his heart pounding.

"Nice catch!" Sofia said. "Your turn. You keep the boat steady while I make a few notes."

She pulled out a small notebook and a pencil

from a waterproof bag that sat under her feet. "I'm keeping a list of all the birds we see today."

"That's just what a scientist would do," Aunt Charlie said. "Some birders even have a 'life list' of all the species they've ever spotted. Look! There's another one!"

Sam and Sofia glanced up and saw a small glossy black bird swoop by before landing in some reeds along the shore.

"Oh!" Sofia gasped excitedly. "What is it?"

"See those red and yellow patches on the bird's shoulders?" Janine asked, pointing at the bird with a twirl of her paddle. "It's a red-winged blackbird. They live in marshy areas."

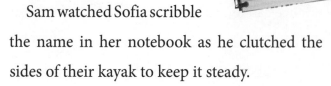

Sam watched Sofia scribble the name in her notebook as he clutched the sides of their kayak to keep it steady.

"Conk-la-reeee! Conk-la-reeee!" the bird squawked at them.

Sam jumped nervously.

Janine laughed. "That's a male," she said. "They always have a lot to say!"

As Sam and Sofia continued to paddle, the wind picked up, pushing them along. A strong gust caught them by surprise, and the kayak tilted to the left. But Sam and Sofia both began to paddle on the right and the boat was soon steady.

Sam let out a huge sigh of relief.

"Kayaking isn't as easy as I thought it would be," he admitted to Sofia.

"True, but it is just as fun as I imagined!" Sofia said. "Look, there's another bird! Quick, take a picture so we can ask Janine what it is."

Sam reached for his camera. As he did, though, his paddle splashed down loudly, scaring off

7

the bird. The camera smacked back into place around his neck.

Sam groaned. "Now we won't know what kind of bird it was."

"See something interesting?" Janine asked as she pulled up alongside Sam and Sofia.

"A light gray bird just flew by," Sofia said. "We wanted to know what type it was."

"Can you describe it to me?" Janine asked.

"It had a bright orange beak that looked as though its tip had been dipped in black paint," Sam said.

"Good eye for detail," Janine said. "That sounds like a common tern. Want to know a fun fact? Unlike humans, they can drink both salt water and fresh water."

Sofia scribbled the name of the bird in her notebook.

"Fantastic!" she exclaimed. "I added three new birds to my list today."

Sam was still thinking about how he had missed his chance to photograph the tern as he buckled his seat belt in Aunt Charlie's car a few minutes later. If only he had been a more confident kayaker, he might not have scared off the bird!

Sam took off his camera and put it on the seat next to his tablet with a small sigh. It would have been nice to have a picture of each bird to go along with Sofia's list.

*Oh well*, Sam thought to himself. *Better luck next time.*

As Aunt Charlie pulled out of the parking lot, Sam's tablet began to chime. He had set it to sound like a bird, and the sound made him smile.

"Oh! It's a video call from my pen pal from school, Cheung!" he said excitedly. "He's calling from China."

Sam picked up the tablet and tapped to answer the call. Cheung's smiling face appeared, his dark hair falling into his eyes.

"Hey, Sam!" Cheung said.

"Hi!" Sam replied.

"Are you in a car?" Cheung asked.

"Yes, but I'm not driving!" Sam said, laughing. "I'm with my friend Sofia. We just went kayaking."

Sam swung his tablet around so Cheung could see Sofia. She beamed and waved.

"Hi, Sofia!" Cheung said. "Kayaking sounds like fun. I'm doing something like that this afternoon because today is Duanwu jie."

"Duanwu jie?" Sam asked, curious. "What's that?"

"Dragon Boat Festival," Cheung replied. "Some people call it Double Fifth Day because of where it falls on the lunar calendar; today is the fifth day of the fifth month! Everyone gets together to race dragon boats and eat sticky rice dumplings. It's really fun!"

"Wow, a boat race!" Sam exclaimed. "Cool!"

"Well, it's usually really fun," Cheung added, frowning. "But today we have a problem—two of our crew members can't be there for the race!"

"I'm sorry," Sam said sympathetically. "I hope you can find some new paddlers."

"Me too," Cheung sighed. "If only you two could join us."

Sam felt Sofia's elbow nudge him in his side.

"I mean, wouldn't it be incredible if this tablet could transport you both here for the race?" Cheung asked, laughing.

"Sam!" Sofia whispered, her eyes sparkling. "Are you thinking what I'm thinking?"

# 2

# An Exciting Invitation

**S**am looked at Sofia. "Us, in a race?" he asked.

But before Cheung could reply, his face froze on the screen.

"Oh no," Sam groaned. "Bad connection."

"If you give it a second, maybe it will unfreeze," Sofia said hopefully. But instead, the screen went black.

"Or that might happen," Sam grumbled, running his fingers through his hair in frustration.

"That's okay," Sofia said, lowering her voice. "We have all the info we need, Sam. If we can get to China, we can help Cheung!"

Sam put a finger to his lips and pointed to his aunt in the front seat. But she was busy humming along to the music on the radio. Sam knew exactly what they needed to do, but he wasn't sure he could. Was he good enough to paddle in a race? Based on his recent kayaking experience, he wasn't so sure.

Sam glanced over at Sofia. She was so excited she was tapping her foot nonstop in anticipation. Her enthusiasm was infectious. Sofia was always up for an adventure, and in his heart, Sam was too. Plus, he really wanted to help Cheung. Maybe this boat race was just the thing to make him a more confident paddler! Sam knew he had to at least give it a try.

As soon as Aunt Charlie pulled into the driveway, Sam hopped out of the back seat, Sofia right behind him.

"What are you two up to?" Aunt Charlie asked as she unlocked the front door to the house she and Sam shared.

"We had an idea for a . . . um, a new project," Sam said quickly. "Can we use some supplies from your lab?"

"Of course," Aunt Charlie replied, stifling a huge yawn. "That kayaking trip wore me out. I'm going to take a quick nap."

Aunt Charlie winked at Sam as she headed upstairs to rest.

"To the lab!" Sofia urged.

Sam and Sofia hurried to the garage, which

Aunt Charlie had transformed into a top-of-the-line science laboratory. Sam's aunt spent much of her time here, concocting new gadgets and amazing scientific inventions. Her most incredible brainchild was sitting in the corner of the lab, cloaked in an oversize tarp.

Sam headed straight for the invention. He grabbed a corner of the tarp and pulled it off.

## Swoosh!

Sam unveiled a shimmering ruby-red scooter. This was no ordinary scooter, though. It had room for two passengers, a  secret compartment for stashing extra supplies, and the power to transport him and Sofia anywhere in the world.

Sofia leaned over and tapped the sleek touch screen mounted on the scooter's handlebars. It lit up with a soft, inviting glow.

"Let's do this!" Sofia said. "Do you know where Cheung lives?"

"He's in Hangzhou," Sam replied. Then he pulled an envelope out of his messenger bag. "Here's one of the letters he sent me."

"Great!" Sofia replied.

Sam climbed onto the scooter and Sofia hopped on behind him. As soon as they were seated, a spinning globe appeared on the screen along with some familiar bright letters.

HELLO EXPLORERS!

Where would you like to travel?

Sam glanced down at the envelope and tapped Cheung's address in Hangzhou, China, into the touch screen.

The globe on the screen expanded, highlighting southeastern China. A blinking blue dot appeared on the east-central coast, just southwest of Shanghai.

"Ready?" Sam asked, his finger poised over the green button that flashed on the screen.

"I sure am," Sofia exclaimed, her voice bubbling with excitement. "*Vamos!*"

Sam inhaled deeply and tapped the button.

"We're off to our first ever dragon boat race!" he cried, gripping the handlebars as the touch screen glowed brightly and the scooter started to vibrate. The headlamps and taillights splashed beams of light onto the garage walls that surrounded them. A moment later, a sparkling corona enveloped the scooter in a dazzling burst of light. Sam squeezed his eyes shut.

## Whiz . . . Zoom . . . FOOP!

# 3

# Welcome to China

**W**hen the scooter stopped rumbling, Sam slowly opened his eyes to find that Aunt Charlie's lab had disappeared. He and Sofia were on a narrow road lined with small buildings and lush green plants. In the distance, a giant multistory pagoda towered over a grove of emerald-green trees. They were in China!

"Wow!" Sam gasped as he slid off the seat. No matter how many times he and Sofia traveled on the scooter, it was always a jaw-dropping experience to be transported to the other side of the world in a heartbeat. He pulled out his camera and pointed it at the impressive pagoda. The many layers made the building look like a magically oversize wedding cake.

## Click-click!

When Sam lowered his camera, he noticed a boy standing outside a small stone building. He was hanging a bouquet of green plants covered in tiny white flowers on the front doorknob.

"Cheung?" Sam asked. "Is that you?"

The boy looked up.

"Sam?!" he exclaimed. "Sofia? You're here! You didn't tell me you were coming."

"Um, it was a surprise?" Sam said.

"Yes! Surprise!" Sofia added.

She and Sam threw open their arms in dramatic reveal poses. Cheung laughed.

"It turns out we weren't too far away when you called us," Sam explained. "So we came here on our scooter to join your dragon boat team!"

"That's incredible!" Cheung exclaimed. "You were already in China?"

"It's so great to see you!" Sam said, quickly changing the subject.

"You too!" Cheung agreed. He still seemed shocked that Sam and Sofia were standing in front of him. "I can't believe you're really here."

"We thought you could use some help in the race?" Sofia said.

"Oh wow, yes!" Cheung said, his face lighting up. "This is great. It would be amazing to have you both on our dragon boat crew!"

"We're in," Sofia said.

"What type of flower is that?" Sam asked, pointing to the bouquet Cheung had just hung on the door. "I've never seen it before."

"This is mugwort," Cheung replied. "During the Dragon Boat Festival, it's tradition to hang it on your door or windows to bring good luck." He pulled two stems of mugwort from the bouquet and handed them to Sam and Sofia.

"There!" he said brightly.

Sam and Sofia tucked the fragrant plant into their pockets. Sam thought about his wobbly kayaking. He could use the extra luck!

A woman with wavy chin-length hair and

glasses poked her head out the front door.

"*Nǐ hǎo*, Mama!" Cheung said. "I hung the mugwort."

"*Xiè xie nǐ!*" Cheung's mother replied. "Who are your friends?"

"This is Sam and his friend Sofia," Cheung introduced them. "This is my mother. You can call her Auntie Min."

"Sam, your pen pal?" she asked.

"They came for a surprise visit!" Cheung said.

Sam and Sofia struck their open-arm pose again, wiggling their fingers.

"How wonderful," Cheung's mother replied. She smiled warmly at Sam and Sofia. "Did you come to watch the boat race?"

"Even better," Cheung said. "They're joining the team. I was just going to show them Bàba's workshop."

"Glad to have you," Min said. "I hope you'll have time after the race for tea and *zòng zi.*"

22

Sam was about to ask Cheung what *zòng zi* was, but Cheung was already motioning for Sam to follow him.

"*Zài jiàn,* Mama!" Cheung called out. His mom gave a wave before she ducked back inside.

Cheung eagerly led Sam and Sofia around the back of the house to a small building with a red-painted door.

"Here we are," Cheung said. "My dad is an artist. He carves dragon heads out of wood and paints them bright colors. Then the heads are mounted onto long boats like sampans to turn them into dragon boats!"

Cheung rapped on the door three times. "Bàba?" he called.

"*Shì de, jìn lái!*" came a friendly voice.

Cheung opened the door. The smell of freshly cut wood filled Sam's nose as he and Sofia followed Cheung inside. Sam's feet crunched on the curly wood shavings that carpeted the floor.

In the center of the room, there was a large worktable with a wooden dragon head sitting on it. A man with unruly hair and a thin mustache stood at the table, adding some details to the dragon with bright green paint.

"Bàba, we have the last two paddlers for our team!" Cheung said. "These are my friends Sam and Sofia. This is my *baba*. You can call him Uncle Wang."

"*Nà tài bàng le!*" Cheung's dad exclaimed. "That's great! Nice to meet you both, and glad to have two more rowers."

"Nice to meet you too," Sam said. He couldn't keep his eyes off the elaborate dragon head. The dragon's mouth was open wide in a sharp-toothed grin, and its head was painted in bright greens and gold. "There's just one more thing that has to happen before I'm done," Cheung's dad said mysteriously. He lowered his voice to a whisper. "We need to awaken the dragon."

25

# 4

## Paint Problems

**S**am glanced at Sofia. What did that mean?
Cheung smiled as if reading Sam's mind.
"Awakening the dragon is the final step before
the dragon is ready to race," he explained. "Once
the head is mounted on the boat, its eyes are

painted red to bring good luck in the race. Once the eyes are on—"

"The dragon is awake!" Sam finished.

Cheung's dad nodded in agreement.

"It's a very important step," he said seriously, though his eyes twinkled merrily as he spoke and his lips twitched into a smile beneath his mustache. "I'll never forget my first dragon boat race when I was a boy. My friends and I were so excited about the race, we forgot to dot the eyes. The race began—1,200 meters through the famous Xixi National Wetland Park—and we were doing great."

Cheung's father grabbed a broom from the corner of the shop and hopped on top of a stool. Then he used the broom to paddle enthusiastically as he told the story.

"The crowd was cheering and the drum was pounding—boom, boom, boom, boom," Wang Lei continued. "I was paddling as fast as I could!"

Cheung chuckled.

"Bàba loves telling this story," he whispered. "I've heard it a thousand times!"

Sam and Sofia leaned forward, eager to hear the rest of the tale.

"Our boat cut through the dark green water," Cheung's father continued, dropping the broom and using his hands to slice through the air. "We were in first place! The finish line was just ahead, and we raised our paddles over our heads in triumph, cheering loudly."

He jumped down off the stool and raised his arms in victory.

"But at that moment, a few paddlers leaned to the left," Cheung's dad said dramatically. "The boat tipped, dumping us all into the river!"

Cheung laughed as Sam and Sofia gasped.

28

"Oh, don't worry," Cheung's dad replied with a chuckle. "Everyone was okay. It happens sometimes, and we all knew how to swim. But to this day, I'm sure I know why we tipped. It was because we forgot to awaken the dragon! If we had dotted the eyes with red paint, we might have had good luck instead of bad!"

"Yikes," Sam said nervously. "I guess we'd better make sure we dot this dragon's eyes if we don't want to tip in the race today!"

Cheung's dad smiled and nodded knowingly. "It's true," he said. "I learned my lesson. Now I never consider a dragon head complete until the eyes have been dotted."

As his dad finished his story, Cheung crossed the small workshop and opened a cabinet wedged in a corner. He rummaged inside, looking for something.

 Finally, he pulled out a small bottle of paint, unscrewed the cap, and turned it upside down. "Bàba," he said in alarm. "There isn't a single drop of red left!"

"*Āi yā!*" Cheung's dad smacked his hand against his forehead in dismay. Then he ran his hand through his hair, making it look even more unruly. "I knew I needed more red paint! I forgot to get it the last time I was at the art supply store."

He turned to Cheung, Sam, and Sofia, and his eyes lit up. "It looks like you three have a special mission. Cheung, you can take the small boat to the art supply store near the Grand Canal. It will be a good chance for you and your friends to practice paddling before the big race!"

He pulled some money out of his pocket and handed a bill to Cheung.

"That should be plenty for paint," he told him.

"I'll meet you at the wetlands just before the race. Good luck!"

"Ready?" Cheung asked Sam and Sofia.

"Definitely!" Sam agreed quickly.

"*Vamos!*" Sofia added, grinning broadly.

Cheung took three paddles that were propped up in a barrel near the door of the workshop. He handed one each to Sofia and Sam. Then he grabbed three bright orange life jackets.

Sam studied the oar in his hands. It was shorter than the one he had used to kayak back home. And it had a blade at just one end and a T shape at the other. His kayaking paddle had blades at both ends.

Cheung led Sam and Sofia from his father's workshop to the riverbank, which ran right alongside his house and yard.

"This is the Yuhangtang River," Cheung explained. "We'll take it to the Grand Canal. Then we'll keep going to the Gongchen Bridge.

We can tie up the boat and cross the bridge on foot. The art store is just on the other side."

Ahead of them, Sam saw a small wooden dock tucked into the river reeds. But the dock was empty and deserted. He looked around, puzzled. Where was the boat Cheung's dad had mentioned?

Cheung took one look at the empty dock and his face fell.

"The boat's gone!" he groaned. "It looks like Mei has struck again!"

# 5

# On the Grand Canal

Sam and Sofia exchanged a glance. Who was Mei? Cheung noticed the confused look on his friends' faces.

"I should explain," he said quickly. "Mei is my neighbor—and my friend. This is the first year she's paddling too, but her family's boat won last year. I'm not sure of the English word, but we have a sort of competition between us."

"Oh, like a rivalry?" Sofia guessed.

"Exactly!" Cheung replied. "Mei plays pranks on me. Her favorite one is to move my boat and tie it a little way down the river."

"What's that?" Sofia asked, pointing to a piece of white paper stuck between two wooden boards on the dock.

Sam bent down to pick it up. He unfolded the paper to reveal a few lines of Chinese characters. He handed the paper to Cheung.

"Well, well," Cheung chuckled. "It looks like Mei left us a clue! This says: Take ten steps to the left or twenty to the right, and you'll find your boat hiding in plain sight!"

"I like her already," Sofia said. "Sam, you go left and Cheung and I will go right. Let's find that boat so we can get the red paint!"

Sam began to count his steps as he walked along the riverbank. It was thick with green reeds and tangles  of vines and shrubs. When Sam had taken his tenth step, he pushed aside a clump of leaves to find the bow of a small canoe!

"Here!" Sam called out. "I think I found it!"

A minute later, Sofia and Cheung came crashing through the foliage.

"Yes!" Cheung shouted when he saw the boat. Mei had tied it securely to the branch of a small tree growing alongside the river.

Cheung untied the boat as Sam and Sofia slipped into their life jackets. Then Sam climbed into the boat. It wobbled a bit from side to side, and Sam sat down quickly behind Cheung while Sofia got in behind him.

"Bàba is the steersperson. That means he stands at the back of the boat and steers during the race," Cheung explained. "Bàba and the drummer, Fen, will shout commands as we go. The first one is 'Sit ready!' Sit up straight holding your paddle and prepare for the next command."

Sam and Sofia both imitated Cheung, sitting up straight with their paddles ready to go.

"That's it!" Cheung said encouragingly. "Be sure to use your feet to anchor yourself in the boat. After that, you'll hear 'Paddles up!' That means you rotate and stretch forward, holding the paddle up and out in front of you."

Sam pressed his feet firmly into the bottom of the boat. He immediately felt more secure. Then he leaned forward with his paddle.

"Perfect!" Cheung told them. "Next you'll hear 'Go!' or 'Take it away!' That means you begin paddling by pulling back toward your hip. Try it!"

Sam and Sofia tried to paddle just the way Cheung had explained it.

"This isn't too hard," Sofia said. "It's different than kayaking, but the goal is the same."

"Keep the boat moving forward, and don't tip over!" Sam said with a laugh. Cheung's paddling tips had helped. Sam was feeling more confident.

"That's right!" Cheung agreed. "Our dragon boat will have 10 paddlers, so it won't be up to just us. We'll go as fast as we can. If everyone paddles to the beat of Fen's drum, we could win!"

Sam took in the scenery around them as they paddled. Small houses and buildings lined the shore as they turned from the river and entered the Grand Canal. Up ahead, Sam could see a tall stone bridge with three arches stretching across the river. There were silhouettes of people walking across the bridge in both directions.

"That's Gongchen Bridge." Cheung pointed to the stone structure. "It's almost 400 years old!"

They pulled up to a small dock crammed with other boats like theirs. Sam and Sofia hopped out behind Cheung.

"Wow, 400 years?" Sam asked as Cheung secured the boat. "Imagine what life was like back then."

"It must have been so different," Cheung said, leading them over the arch of stone, "but people walked over this same bridge to cross the canal."

Around them, the banks were packed with people on foot and on bicycles. Sam paused briefly at the top of the bridge to catch his breath.

"Come on!" Cheung called back to Sam. "We're almost there!"

Then he led the way downhill toward the other side of the river.

# 6

# The Streets of Hangzhou

Cheung darted between the crowds of people strolling and shopping. He was moving so quickly, Sam was afraid he and Sofia wouldn't be able to keep up. Suddenly, Sam panicked and froze. What if the same thing happened in the boat? What if he wasn't able to paddle fast enough?

"Sam?" Sofia asked. "Are you okay?"

"Oh yeah," Sam said, forcing a smile. "Just thinking about something else."

Cheung circled back and led them forward. "Sorry I lost you," he said. "It's so crowded today. The paint store is right over here."

He gestured toward a small doorway and ducked inside. Sam and Sofia followed.

The store was cool and quiet and empty. Sam looked around at the shelves lined with containers and jars of paint and paintbrushes of all shapes and sizes. There were racks of canvases and workbooks around the edges of the store, and pyramids stacked with notebooks and drawing paper in the center.

"What a great shop!" Sam exclaimed.

"It smells just like my *papai's* studio," Sofia said, inhaling deeply. "He's an artist too."

Cheung carefully examined the jars lining the shelves. Finally, he snagged a red one.

"This is it!" he said. At that moment, a woman emerged from the back of the shop.

"*Nǐ hǎo*, Cheung!" she said brightly.

"*Nǐ hǎo*, Auntie Hai Rong," Cheung replied. "These are my friends, Sam and Sofia. This is Mei's aunt. She owns the shop."

"Hello and welcome," Auntie Hai Rong said. "Any friends of Mei are friends of mine. How do you know her?"

"Well, we haven't met yet," Sam replied. "But we'll see her later today at the dragon boat race."

"Ah, of course!" Hai Rong exclaimed. "Mei has been training hard. She really wants to win the race. And I'm sure you want to win too."

"We do!" Cheung said, nodding eagerly.

"My niece won't make it easy for you!" Hai Rong said. She waggled her eyebrows at Cheung.

Cheung laughed as he paid for the paint.

"Good luck," she told Cheung playfully. "You'll need it!"

"*Xiè xie nī!*" Cheung said as he grabbed the bag and waved goodbye on his way out.

"Mei's aunt made the race sound so . . . intense," Sam said once they were outside. "Is it?"

"Auntie Hai Rong is a lot like Mei," Cheung said. "She loves to tease! Some people take the race really seriously, but most of us just want to have a good time. I promise you'll have fun."

Then Cheung glanced at his watch. "Now we'd better hurry back. The race starts in less than an hour!"

# 7

## Meeting Mei

Back at Cheung's house, Sam and Sofia climbed out of the boat and helped tie it up while Cheung checked the time again.

"We have thirty minutes to get to the Xixi Wetlands," he said. "I can usually bike there in about twenty minutes, but I only have one bike."

"Not a problem," Sofia said quickly. "We have our scooter, remember?"

"That's right!" Cheung said happily.

The three friends hurried over to the scooter, which they'd parked near Cheung's blue bicycle.

"Actually," Sam said, "we can all take the scooter!" He felt his mouth twitch into a smile.

"We can?" Cheung asked. "It looks like only two people will fit."

"That's true, if we're driving the scooter on the street," Sofia confided. "But all three of us can squeeze on if we use the special touch screen."

Cheung looked confused.

"What do you mean?" he asked.

"Can you keep a secret?" Sam whispered.

"Of course," Cheung replied.

"My aunt is an inventor," Sam explained. "She designed and built the scooter to travel around the world. It transports people instantly. It's the smartest form of transportation ever created!"

"Are you kidding?!" Cheung asked, his voice full of disbelief.

"Nope," Sofia replied, shaking her head. "When you said you wished we were here to row in your dragon boat, we used the scooter to bring us here to China!"

Cheung's jaw dropped open. "That's how you got here so quickly?"

He ran his hand over the smooth, sleek machine, but he still looked skeptical.

"But how does it work?" he asked.

"We're not exactly sure," Sam admitted. "We type in the place we want to go, and it takes us there in seconds."

"That sounds incredible!" Cheung said. He still didn't look convinced, though. "I can see why you might not want everyone to know about that."

"We trust you," Sam said.

"So what do you say?" Sofia asked Cheung. "Want to see for yourself?"

Cheung broke into a huge grin. "Of course!"

"*Vamos!*" Sofia said.

Sam and Sofia climbed onto the sparkling red scooter. Cheung was just about to climb onto the scooter behind Sofia when he was startled by the sound of bike tires on gravel.

Cheung whirled around. "Mei!" he cried.

Sam and Sofia looked over and saw a rosy-cheeked girl in a blue T-shirt with a long, dark ponytail perched on a red bicycle. The bicycle matched the color of their red scooter perfectly.

"Who are your friends?" Mei asked brightly.

Cheung introduced Sam and Sofia. "You heading to the race?" he asked.

Mei nodded. "And it looks like I'd better hurry."

She pushed off with one foot and started to pedal. Then she called back over her shoulder, her voice a teasing singsong. "Your red scooter might get you to the starting line faster than my bike," she said, "but our boat will cross the finish line first. Just you wait and see!"

She tossed her ponytail over her shoulder and sped off, pedaling furiously. As soon as Mei was out of sight, Cheung hopped on the scooter.

"Let's do this!" he said.

"Here we go," Sam said as he typed in their destination.

**Whiz . . . Zoom . . . FOOP!**

# 8

# The Lion Dance

**W**hen the blinding light had faded and the scooter stopped rumbling, Sam, Sofia, and Cheung found themselves on a stone pathway near a small wooden bridge, surrounded by emerald-green water. Luckily, there was no one else around.

"Wow!" Cheung gasped as he climbed off the scooter and looked around, his eyes wide with surprise. "Did that really happen?!"

Sam nodded.

"Incredible, isn't it?" he asked. "I couldn't believe it the first time either."

"Oh good!" Cheung said with a shaky laugh. "I really thought you were just joking around. I went along to see what would happen, but I didn't expect that. I mean . . . wow! That was amazing!"

Cheung shook his head again.

"You've shown us so many cool things on this trip, we're glad we could do the same!" Sam said.

"Now if only our dragon boat could move that fast, we'd be across the finish line in no time!" Cheung replied with a laugh.

"Maybe Aunt Charlie's next extraordinary invention should be in boat form," Sofia said.

"That would be something," Cheung said. Then he glanced at his watch again.

"Yikes!" he said. "We really have to hurry. The race starts in less than 10 minutes! This way!"

Sam and Sofia followed Cheung over the small bridge. The wooden walkway wound its way through the verdant green wetlands. There was water on either side of them, and thriving plants and bushes grew at every turn.

As Sofia hurried, she tried to take in the beautiful scenery around her.

"Sam, doesn't this area remind you of our kayaking trip back home?" she asked.

Sam nodded. "Definitely," he agreed. "There were a lot of plants in the marsh too, and we even spotted those cool birds, remember?"

"Yes!" Sofia said softly. "And speaking of birds, look over there!"

She pointed to an unusual-looking bird with a white body and a long, feathery tail that was marked with interesting black triangles. The bird was half hidden in some foliage, but its bright red face and legs were the same color red as the paint they had just bought.

"Oh wow!" Cheung said when he saw the bird. "That's a silver pheasant. They live around here, but I don't see them often. They were special birds in ancient China, and seeing one is a sign of good fortune!"

Sofia excitedly pulled a small notebook out of her pocket.

"Awesome," she said. Then she quickly jotted down the name. "I'll add it to my bird life list!"

Sam pulled out his camera and snapped a quick photo.

## Click-click!

- Pelican
- Wood duck
- Mallard
(fancy duck with green neck!)
- Egret
- Great blue heron
- Red-winged blackbird
- Silver pheasant

Sam was reminded of the last time he had stopped what he was doing to take a photo of a bird—and almost lost his kayak paddle in the bay! He took a few deep breaths to calm his nerves.

*You can do this*, Sam thought to himself. He closed his eyes and pictured himself staying cool and calm during the race. He was visualizing their boat gliding across the finish line when Sofia interrupted his thoughts.

"Sam, come on!" she said. She pointed at Cheung, who was way ahead of them.

Sam quickly hurried after his friends. He soon began to hear the faint buzzing sounds of a crowd. A moment later, he rounded one last curve in the walkway and found himself on a large dock packed with people. A line of dragon boats sat in the water, some full of paddlers and some still empty.

Cheung opened his mouth to say something, but his words were drowned out by a sudden loud gong followed by a drum and clanging cymbals. A small group of musicians appeared on the dock. Their colorful orange shirts were paired with loose red knee-length pants decorated with intricately painted pink flowers.

The drumming and clanging continued, and suddenly two fuzzy lions emerged from the crowd. They had oversized heads with giant cartoonish eyes and sparkly bodies covered in flowing gold and white ruffles.

"It's the lion dance!" Cheung shouted over the cymbals and drums. "The noisy music is supposed to scare away bad spirits and bring good luck before the race. There are two dancers inside each costume—one controls the front legs, head, eyes, and mouth, and the other moves the lion's back legs. Lion dancers celebrate Chinese New Year, and we invite them to the boat festival too."

Sam and Sofia watched as the mischievous costumed lions danced around the dock to the beat.

Sam became caught up in the dancers' mesmerizing movements. He forgot that he was watching two people performing a skillful dance. Instead, it felt as though he were really watching two giant lions prancing across the dock! Sam couldn't explain it if he tried, but the loud drums, clanging cymbals, and the playful lions filled him with a sense of joy and delight.

Suddenly the knot of nerves in his stomach loosened and he felt ready for the competition. No matter the outcome, Sam was determined to have fun as he paddled in his first ever dragon boat race.

"Let's look for my dad," Cheung called out over the music. "The lion dance means it's almost time to dot the dragon's eyes."

Sam stood on his tiptoes and scanned the faces in the crowd, but he didn't see Wang Lei anywhere. As he looked, he didn't realize that the dancers had come up right behind him. A lion's head bobbed above him, and the lion blinked its large eyes at him, batting its eyelashes and opening and closing its mouth playfully.

Cheung quickly pulled a red envelope from his pocket and slipped it into Sam's hand.

"The lion is hungry," Cheung explained quickly, his eyes sparkling merrily. "This envelope is called a *hóng bāo*. It contains a gift of money. It's good luck to feed the envelope to the lion before our race!"

Sam took the envelope. Now that he knew what to do, he was excited to feed the giant lion! Sam held out the envelope to the dancers, and

the frisky, spirited lion reared up on its hind legs. The crowd cheered approvingly.

Flushed with excitement, Sam reached up and slipped the red envelope into the lion's mouth. The clanging cymbals and drums grew even louder and Cheung gave an enthusiastic thumbs-up.

Then Cheung passed a red envelope to Sofia.

Sam pulled out his camera to snap a photo of Sofia feeding her envelope to the lion.

### Click-click!

Sofia burst out laughing when the lion bowed down to her in thanks afterward.

"Nice work, you two," came a voice from behind Sam. He whirled around to see that Cheung's dad had found them in the crowd.

"Do you think you're up for one more task before the race?" Cheung's dad asked Sam and Sofia.

# 9

# Awakening the Dragon

"It's time to dot the dragon's eyes, and since you two helped on the paint mission, I think you should have the honor," Cheung's dad told them.

"Really?!" Sam gasped in surprise. He was

thrilled to have the chance to paint part of the spectacular dragon head.

"Of course," Cheung's dad replied with a grin.

"We would love to do it," Sofia said quickly, and Sam nodded in agreement.

Cheung removed the jar of paint from his backpack. Meanwhile, his dad produced two small paintbrushes and handed one each to Sam and Sofia.

"All you have to do is dot each of the dragon's eyes with a bit of red paint," Wang Lei explained. "That will awaken the dragon from its slumber so it's ready to race!"

Cheung held out the paint, and Sam dipped his paintbrush in. Sofia did the same.

"On the count of three," Cheung said. "One . . . two . . . THREE!"

At the same time, Sam and Sofia dabbed their brushes against the dragon's black pupils. The crowd cheered wildly.

"Now that the last dragon is officially awake, the race can begin," Cheung's dad announced to the crowd. He carefully picked up the dragon head and placed it on the front of the long boat that was waiting in the water.

Everyone on the dock moved toward their dragon boats and climbed in. Cheung's dad held their boat steady while the team loaded from the middle. As everyone climbed aboard, Cheung quickly introduced Sam and Sofia to the rest of the crew.

"This is Jin and his father, Shu-hui," Cheung said as a boy about his age climbed into the boat along with a man with the same wavy hair and bright smile. "They live really close to me."

"*Nǐ hǎo,*" Sam greeted the pair.

Next, two identical girls with matching pixie haircuts climbed into the long boat.

"These are the twins, Ling and Yan," Cheung said. "They go to school with me."

One girl was quiet and had a serious look on her face, while the other grinned at Sam and Sofia.

"Hi!" she said. "Thanks for joining our team!"

Finally, a family wearing matching red T-shirts climbed into the boat.

"And this is Bo, Liang, and their daughter Genji," Cheung said. "They live in my neighborhood too. Liang is an amazing paddler. If you're not sure what to do, just watch her."

"Nice to meet you!" Genji said to Sam. "Hope you're ready to race. It's going to be so much fun!"

Sam, Sofia, and Cheung climbed into the boat after Genji and took their places. Cheung sat next to his dad, and Sam and Sofia were right in front of them.

"The drummer is Liang's sister, Fen," Cheung explained. "Do you remember the commands I taught you earlier?"

"Yup, definitely!" Sofia said confidently.

Sam hesitated. "I think so," he replied, suddenly nervous again.

"Don't worry," Cheung reassured him. "If you forget, just follow me or Liang. And remember to have fun!"

The boats around them filled up with paddlers and drummers. Cheung glanced around the dock, a worried look on his face. Sofia could sense something was bothering him.

"What's wrong?" she asked as she steadied herself in the boat with her feet.

"I don't see Mei yet," Cheung replied anxiously. "I don't want her to miss the start!"

"It wouldn't be much fun if she didn't get to race," Sam agreed.

He and Sofia searched the dock, but they didn't see Mei anywhere.

"First three seats, give me three strokes," Cheung's dad called out. Jin, Shu-hui,

Ling, Yan, Bo, and Genji paddled together to move the boat so that it was lined up with the others at the starting line.

"All boats hold!" came the loud voice of the referee.

"The race is about to start," Cheung said nervously.

At that moment, Sam caught sight of a bright orange life vest and a long, dark ponytail. It was Mei! She came sprinting across the dock and hopped into the  boat beside theirs. She turned to Cheung, Sam, and Sofia and gave them a quick wave before picking up her paddle. Cheung grinned happily.

"We have alignment!" the referee called. "Drummers, are you ready?"

"This is it," Cheung whispered excitedly.

"Sit ready!" Cheung's dad called out, and Sam,

Sofia, Cheung, Liang, and the rest of the crew got into their starting positions.

"Paddles up!" Cheung's dad shouted as a horn blasted. "And . . . GO!"

# 10

# Race to the Finish

Sam dipped his paddle into the water with a splash. The boat lurched forward quickly, wobbling back and forth as the ten paddlers worked to get up to speed. The boat moved forward, slicing through the water.

Fen pounded on the drum as she shouted along to the beat. "One, two, three, four, five," she called. "Up, up, up, four, five, six, seven, eight, nine, ten. One, two, three, four, five, six, seven, eight, nine, ten!"

Sam followed Cheung and Liang, doing his best to keep time with Cheung's paddle. Still, it was tough. But Sam was determined to try his best and have fun. He noticed that the butterflies in his stomach had settled down and he was focused on just one goal—reaching the finish line first! Sam glanced to his left for a moment and noticed that Mei's boat was right alongside theirs. In fact, as soon as Sam noticed Mei, her boat seemed to pull ahead.

### Boom! Boom! Boom!

Fen banged the drum loudly as Sam, Sofia, Cheung, Liang, and the rest of the team paddled along to the beat.

"Come on!" Cheung's dad called out as the

gap between their boat and Mei's widened. "Stay strong and keep paddling!"

Sam could feel his arms growing heavy and his lungs burning as he lifted his paddle up and down over and over again.

"Wow," he gasped between strokes. "This is hard work!"

"You're doing great," Cheung called back encouragingly. "Just keep paddling!"

Next to Sam, Sofia had a determined look on her face. She glanced at Mei and caught the girl's eye. Mei grinned and then seemed to dig her paddle into the river with renewed energy.

## Boom! Boom! Boom!

The drum continued to pound, and Sam suddenly noticed the crowds of people along the shore, cheering and waving wildly as the boats went by. Their enthusiastic shouts made Sam's arms tingle with a fresh wave of energy. He paddled harder and faster than he ever had before. Slowly, he noticed their boat inching closer and closer to Mei's. Sam dug deep and paddled even harder.

"How much farther to the finish line?" he asked Cheung.

"It's just ahead!" came Cheung's reply. Fen began to push the pace, beating the drum faster and faster. Sam noticed Cheung and Liang increase the speed of their paddling to keep up.

"We've got this!" Cheung shouted. "Let's go!"

Sam and Sofia lowered their heads and gave it their all. Their paddles flew as water splashed into the boat, soaking their T-shirts and shorts.

Sam glanced up for a moment and saw that they had caught up with Mei's boat and were pulling ahead! Mei seemed to sense this, though, and she shouted at her crewmates. They increased their pace and began to move to the front again.

"No way, Mei!" Cheung shouted playfully to his friend. "You're not going to win this one!"

## Boom! Boom! Boom!

Sam felt himself slip into a rhythm. He no longer felt tired as he paddled—he felt as though he and the rest of the crew had come together into one unstoppable force. Ahead of him, he spied a line of red buoys in the water marking the finish line.

"Finish!" Cheung's dad called out, alerting them that they were almost there.

Sam was so excited he almost jumped up out of his seat. But he quickly regained his focus, anchoring his feet in the boat, putting down his head, and paddling hard, more determined than ever to finish strong. His paddle flying, Sam saw the red buoys go by out of the corner of his eye.

"Yes!" Cheung, Liang, Jin, Shu-hui, and the

rest of the crew cheered loudly. Cheung pumped his fist in the air. "We did it!"

"We did?" Sam asked, finally looking up as he let his paddle fall into his lap as a wave of exhaustion hit him. He didn't think he had ever felt so tired in his entire life!

"Yes, we won!" Cheung exclaimed, grinning broadly. "You and Sofia were terrific!"

"No way," Sam said bashfully, though his cheeks were flushed with pride. "We only helped a little bit."

"It's . . . true," Sofia gasped between breaths. "Dragon boat racing is a lot harder than it looks!"

"You two really came through," Cheung said. "We couldn't have done it without ten paddlers in the boat. Every member of the crew was important. Thank you again!"

Sam leaned back and closed his eyes, taking deep breaths and enjoying the sensation of having won the race. What a feeling!

"Look!" Sofia said suddenly.

Sam's eyes flew open. He saw Sofia pointing to a small white bird with black legs and yellow feet standing on the shore. It had just plucked a tiny fish from the river, which it held tightly in its black bill as the fish thrashed around.

"That's a little egret," Wang Lei told them. "Egrets are a type of heron. They're a sign of peace, strength, and longevity."

"Another bird for my bird life list!" Sofia crowed. "Sam, remind me to write that one down in my notebook later."

"Looks like you had a good luck charm on your side, Cheung," Mei called from the next boat with a nod to the pretty white bird. She smiled good-naturedly at her friend.

"Great race, Mei," Cheung said graciously. "Next year it will be your boat's turn to win."

"That's if I don't beat you in a bike race before then," came Mei's quick retort. She tossed her ponytail over her shoulder defiantly. "In the meantime, I hope you and your friends will come to my house to celebrate your victory. My mother and grandmother have been making *zòng zi* all day—there's enough to feed about 10 boatloads of guests!"

"Definitely!" Cheung replied. "It wouldn't be a dragon boat race without *zòng zi*. We'll be there!"

# 11
## Sticky Rice Dumplings

The race over, the crew paddled back to the dock. Sam, Sofia, Cheung, and Liang climbed out of the boat along with the rest of the crew, exchanging hugs and high fives. Then everyone worked together to carry the boat from the river to a nearby storage shed.

"Great job today!" Fen told Sam and Sofia. "I've never seen first-time paddlers work so hard."

"Thank you," Sam said. "When the drum sped up, I wasn't sure if I could keep up."

"Well, you did it!" Fen said, smiling. "You should feel proud. Nice work."

"Yes, it was a great race!" Yan agreed. "I'm glad you brought your friends, Cheung."

"Me too," Cheung said. "I can't believe Mei's boat was in the lead the entire time! But we really came through in the end."

"Way to go, team!" Cheung's dad agreed. "And it helped that we remembered to dot the dragon's eyes. Otherwise, who knows how things would have turned out?"

Cheung's dad threw back his head and laughed heartily.

"I'm glad your friends chose today to visit," he

told Cheung. "Now you kids should head home for some *zòng zi*. I'll wipe down the boat and put away the rest of the equipment. I'll be there soon!"

"Thanks, Bàba!" Cheung said. "See you later!"

Then he turned to Sam and Sofia.

"Do you have time for some food before you have to head home?" Cheung asked.

"Are you kidding?" Sam replied. "Of course we do!"

"What are *zòng zi*?" Sofia asked as they hurried back to the scooter.

"They're sticky rice dumplings," Cheung explained. He patted his stomach enthusiastically. "They're soooo good! You add different fillings to the rice, and then it's wrapped up in bamboo leaves and steamed. The ones my mom makes are the best!"

"They sound delicious," Sam agreed. Now that the race was behind him, his appetite was back in full force. His stomach let out a growl.

"We eat *zòng zi* during Dragon Boat Festival to honor Qu Yuan," Cheung continued. "Everyone makes them, but families use different fillings."

"Who is Qu Yuan?" Sofia asked, curious. "I don't think I've heard that name before."

"He's a famous Chinese poet who lived about 2,300 years ago," Cheung explained. "Everyone in China knows who he is."

They arrived back at the scooter to find it was still tucked safely away.

"The faster we get back, the faster we can try these famous dumplings," Sam said as he climbed on the scooter. Sofia and Cheung hopped on behind him, eager to get back to Chueng's house as well.

"Is everyone ready?" Sam asked, tapping the touch screen.

"Yes!" Sofia and Cheung shouted in unison.

**Whiz . . . Zoom . . . FOOP!**

A few seconds later, Sam, Cheung, and Sofia were on Cheung's street again. Cheung hopped off the bike and shook out his arms and legs.

"Wow," he said in awe. "I'll bet that never gets old!"

Sam and Sofia laughed.

"You're right," Sam replied. "It feels like a new adventure every time we ride!"

"Let's head over to Mei's," Cheung said eagerly. "I'm ready to eat!"

Sam, Sofia, and Cheung hurried past Cheung's house. But as they walked by the front door, it flew open. Cheung's mother suddenly popped her head out of the house.

"Cheung!" her voice rang out. "Don't take another step!"

# 12

# Five Strings and a Feast

Sam and Sofia froze in their tracks. Oh no!
Had Cheung's mother seen them on the
scooter? Had their secret been discovered?

"Yes, Mama?" Cheung replied quickly.

"I need some help carrying my *zòng zi* over to

Mei's," came his mother's reply. She was holding a large plate loaded with green triangular packets tied with string.

Cheung laughed, and Sam sighed with relief. Their scooter secret was still safe!

Cheung dashed over to his mother and took the plate.

"Sure, Mama," Cheung said. "I've got this one. No problem."

"Good," Cheung's mother replied. "I have one more plate to prepare. Give me one second and we can all head over together."

"Okay!" Cheung replied.

"I thought Mei's family was making *zòng zi*," Sofia said in surprise. "Your mother made *zòng zi*, too? It sounds like there's going to be a lot of food at Mei's house!"

Cheung laughed again.

"Oh yes," he explained. "It isn't Duanwu jie without a feast. My mother makes *zòng zi* every year. She grew up in northern China. Where she's from, people prefer sweet *zòng zi* filled with things like dates and red beans. But here in southern China, most *zòng zi* are stuffed with foods like mushrooms, fatty pork, and egg."

Sofia eyed the tray.

"So those are sweet *zòng zi*, then?" she asked.

"Yes," Cheung replied, nodding. "But Mei's mother and grandmother grew up here in Hangzhou, so they make savory ones. They have a rivalry with my mom, just like Mei and I competing in the boat race. Every year, they argue over who makes the best sticky rice dumplings."

"Well, I can't wait to taste both!" Sam said.

Cheung's mother emerged from the house again, carrying a second plate stacked high with *zòng zi*.

"Can I help with that?" Sofia asked, motioning to the overflowing plate.

"Oh yes, thank you," Cheung's mother replied. She handed the tray to Sofia.

When the group arrived at Mei's house, Mei raced outside to greet them.

"You're here!" she exclaimed.

Then she grabbed Sam and Sofia's hands and pulled them inside the house. A large table in the center of the room was covered with delicious-smelling dishes.

"*Nǐ hǎo*, Min," an older, gray-haired woman greeted Cheung's mother with a crinkly smile. "I see you've brought your *zòng zi*. They look good, but mine are better!"

"Oh stop, Wài pó," Mei said playfully. "Don't listen to my grandmother. She's only joking!"

Everyone laughed good-naturedly.

"See?" Cheung told Sam and Sofia. "Everyone in Mei's family loves to tease! It's all in good fun, though. All the *zòng zi* are delicious—sweet and salty."

A tall woman with her hair pulled back in a bun entered the room. She was wearing an apron and carrying a plate of *zòng zi*.

"This is my mother," Mei said. "These are Cheung's friends, Sam and Sofia."

"Welcome!" she told Sam and Sofia. "I heard the results of the race. Congratulations!" She motioned to the steaming food. "Now please, sit down. I hope you're all hungry!"

Mei's mother placed two *zòng zi* on each plate and passed them around the table. "First, you have to try Wài pó's salty *zòng zi*. Then you can try Min's sweet one!"

Cheung showed Sam and Sofia how to unwrap each bamboo leaf packet to reveal the steamed sticky rice dumpling inside. Mei picked up a pair of chopsticks and demonstrated the best way to use them.

"You just break the rice apart like this," Mei said. She used her chopstick to dig in to the rice, revealing a fragrant, meaty filling. Then she picked up a piece of pork with the chopsticks and popped it in her mouth.

"Mmmmm," Mei said. "It's delicious, Wài pó!"

Sam and Sofia followed Cheung and Mei's instructions, unwrapping the bamboo leaves to reveal the rice and pork inside.

Sam carefully used his chopsticks to lift a chunk of rice mixed with pork into his mouth.

"Oh wow!" he exclaimed. "That's so good!"

"I'm glad you like it," Mei's grandmother said as she poured steaming hot tea into Sam's cup. "*Zòng zi* are perfect with a cup of dragon well tea."

"What's that?" Sam asked, intrigued. He took a sip of the fragrant drink.

"It's a type of green tea from right here in Hangzhou," Cheung's mother replied. "It has grown in tea plantations in this area for more than 1,200 years."

"I like it," Sofia proclaimed as she sipped the hot, bitter drink.

"You'll like it even more with my sweet *zòng zi*," Cheung's mother replied.

Sam and Sofia moved on to the sticky rice dumpling stuffed with red bean paste.

"Yum!" Sam exclaimed. "It's so good . . . like a delicious dessert!"

"See?" Mei said, laughing as she refilled Sam and Sofia's cups of tea. "Whenever we try to vote on whose *zòng zi* are best, it's always a tie."

Sam could understand why. No matter how much he tried to pick a winner, he liked every *zòng zi* he tasted. It was impossible to choose a favorite. Soon he and Sofia were stuffed with tea and dumplings. Sam didn't think he could eat another bite!

"Thank you for the feast," Sofia said. "It was really delicious."

"I'm so glad you came to visit," Cheung said.

"Me too!" Sam agreed. "But we should probably head home before it gets much later."

"Wait!" Mei cried suddenly. She dashed over to talk with her grandmother. A minute later she returned, handing something to Cheung.

"We have gifts for you," Cheung explained as he held out a colorful braided rope.

"It's a five-color string bracelet," Mei told Sofia. "May I tie it on your wrist?"

"Sure!" Sofia agreed. She pushed up her sleeve and held out her arm.

"This bracelet is a Dragon Boat Festival tradition," Mei said. "Wài pó makes them every year and gives them to the children in the neighborhood. The five colors—green, red, white, black, and yellow—are lucky in China."

"The bracelet is meant to protect you and keep you healthy," Cheung said. "I have one for you too, Sam."

He tied the colorful bracelet on Sam's wrist.

"Thank you!" Sam said. "Now let's get a picture before Sofia and I have to go."

He pulled out his camera.

"Say *zòng zi*!" Sam said, grinning.

"*Zòng zi*!" everyone replied as Sam snapped the selfie.

## Click-click!

"Thanks again for a fantastic adventure and an incredible feast," Sam told Cheung, Mei, and their families. "Please tell your father we loved meeting him and racing in his dragon boat!"

"We'll always remember this trip," Sofia agreed.

"Thank you again for coming," Cheung replied. "And get home safely!"

"I'll write to you soon," Sam told Cheung as he and Sofia headed back outside, where the sun was beginning to set over the treetops. "And I'll send photos!"

"I'm always a little sad when it's time to go home," Sofia said as they returned to the scooter.

"Me too," Sam agreed. "But I know there's always another incredible journey just around the corner!"

He pressed the green button on the touch screen and the bright light from the scooter's headlamps and taillights lit up the stone road in front of them.

"Ready to go?" Sam asked Sofia.

"Ready!" she replied. "*Vamos!*"

**Whiz . . . Zoom . . . FOOP!**

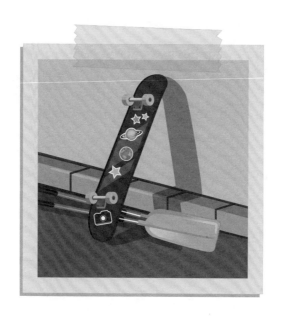

# 13

# Another Adventure Awaits

**A** few seconds later, Sam and Sofia found themselves back in Aunt Charlie's lab. Sam realized he was still wearing his camera around his neck. He took it off and slipped it into his messenger bag. Then he made a mental note to remember to send the photos to Cheung later that evening.

Sam and Sofia were heading out of the lab when Aunt Charlie poked her head in.

"How's the project going?" she asked, smiling encouragingly.

"It's great!" Sofia replied quickly.

"We, uh, just finished up for the day," Sam added.

"Terrific," his aunt replied, patting Sam on the shoulder. Sam's eyes widened in surprise as he realized his T-shirt was still damp from the boat race. "Oh, and Sam? You might want to change before dinner. Your T-shirt is a little wet."

She winked at him playfully.

"Um, yeah, okay," Sam agreed quickly.

*Does she know where we've been?* he wondered. He glanced at Sofia, but she shrugged and raised her eyebrows as if to say she had no idea either.

"And would you mind tidying up the front yard?" Aunt Charlie continued. "Your skateboard and bike are out there, and it looks like it's going to storm tonight."

"Sure thing," Sam replied, and he and Sofia headed outside before Aunt Charlie could say anything else.

"Do you think she knows?" Sofia asked.

"No way," Sam said, but he wasn't so sure. "At least, I don't think so."

When they got outside, Sam picked up his skateboard. As he did, he caught a glimpse of the colorful braided bracelet on his wrist. Suddenly he had an idea.

"Hop into the boat, Sofia!" he cried, gesturing toward his skateboard. Then he grabbed a broom that had been standing against the side of the house and held it like a paddle. Sofia instantly understood what he was doing. She took a seat on the skateboard and Sam stepped onto the board right behind her.

"Sit ready!" he called out jokingly.

"Paddles up!" Sofia replied with a laugh. "And GO!"

Sam began to paddle furiously against the ground with the broom, and he and Sofia zipped down the driveway on the skateboard, cheering loudly.

Aunt Charlie stuck her head out the window.

"What on earth are you two up to?" she asked, her eyes twinkling merrily.

"Just working on our paddling skills!" Sam called back as he and Sofia rolled by, hooting the entire time.

"It's great to see you so confident and excited," Aunt Charlie replied brightly. "Especially because I signed the three of us up for a three-day-long kayaking and camping trip in a few weeks."

"Really?!" Sam asked, a grin spreading across

his face. "All right!"

"Looks like you were right, Sam," Sofia called out from her seat on the skateboard. "We'll be off on another incredible adventure in no time!"

## Jié shù
## (The End)

# Mandarin Terms

- Āi yā! - Oh!

- Bàba - Dad

- Chá - Tea

- Chuán - Boat

- Hé - River

- Lóng - Dragon

- Péng you - Friend

- Wài pó - Grandma

- Yì shù - Art

- Yóu xì - Game

- Zòng zi - Sticky rice dumpling

## Mandarin Phrases

- Nǐ hǎo - Hello

- Nǐ hǎo ma - Hi, how are you?

- Nà tài bàng le - That's great!

- Qǐng xiǎng yòng - Enjoy your meal

- Shì de, jìn lái - Yes, come in

- Xiè xie nī - Thank you

- Zài jiàn - See you again later

## Portuguese Phrase

- Vamos! - Let's go!

# Sofia and Sam's Snippets

China's official name is the People's Republic of China. Beijing is the nation's capital.

More than a billion people live in this beautiful country full of breathtaking sights and rich cultural traditions.

Mountains stretch across one third of China's land, and the Himalayas are the most notable range. Thousands of rivers also snake across the country. The Yangtze River is the third-largest river on Earth, measuring 3,915 miles.

Chinese is one of the oldest written languages in the entire world! Writings have been found dating all the way back to the Shang dynasty, which occurred between 1766 and 1123 BCE. That means Chinese has been written for more than 3,000 years!

There are thousands of characters in the Chinese language. About 2,000 to 4,000 are most often used in everyday speaking, but that's just a fraction! It's also the language with the most native speakers on Earth.

Many groundbreaking inventions were created and developed in China. Chinese inventions include paper, the compass, silk, mechanical clocks, and the world's first seismograph (earthquake detector).

Originating in China, the sport of dragon boat racing is now practiced all over the world. More than 60 countries regularly host dragon boat races, with millions of paddlers participating.

In Chinese mythology, dragons are believed to rule over rivers and rainfall. Displaying ornate dragon heads at the front of boats is a way to honor the powerful beasts.

By respecting them, some believe the dragons respond by preventing droughts and sending rain, making for bountiful rice harvests.

Cheung and Mei's families aren't the only ones with special **zòng zi** recipes. There are more than 20 types of sticky rice dumplings in China, with variations for each recipe. So many flavors to try!

Another of Cheung's favorite snacks is called **cong bao hui**. It's a Hangzhou specialty: a scallion pancake panfried to be crispy on the outside and soft on the inside. The savory morsels are often served with sweet bean sauce or chili sauce.

The Gongchen Bridge is around 400 years old and is the highest and longest stone bridge in Hangzhou. It marks the beginning of the Grand Canal, which connects five river basins in China.

# Five-Color String Bracelet

## Materials:

☐ 20-inch-long pieces of string in:
red, white, black, yellow, and green

☐ 8" x 10" piece of cardboard

☐ Scissors

☐ Tape

Wearing bracelets made of
five strings, one of each
color listed above, is a
popular tradition during
the Dragon Boat Festival.

Together, the five colors are
considered lucky in Chinese culture, and
wearing the bracelet is believed to bring good
fortune and a long healthy life.

Make your own bracelet inspired by Sam and
Sofia's new friends Cheung and Mei!

## Instructions:

**1.** Knot the five strings together at one end.

**2.** Cut a slit at the top and bottom of the cardboard. Wedge the ends above the knot into the top slit and tape to the back of the board.

**3.** Pull four of the strings down across the front of the board and wedge them into the slit at the bottom.

**4.** Drape the loose string across the four anchored strings, creating a D shape. Slide the end of the string beneath the anchored strings, and pull it up through the center of the D-shaped loop. Pull taut, sliding the knot to the top. Repeat until you have about an inch of knots completed.

**A**

**B**

**C**

**5.** Release the four anchored strings, select a new color to keep loose, and anchor the other four strings again. Tie another inch of knots, switch the color again, and so on. Tie the end once you've reached your desired length, and you're done!